This Little Tiger book belongs to:

_____

_____

_____

For Niki and Nelli – N L

For Noah, Levi, Isaac, Daniel, Dylan and Jacob xxxxxx – J C

LITTLE TIGER PRESS
1 The Coda Centre, 189 Munster Road,
London SW6 6AW
www.littletiger.co.uk
First published in Great Britain 2011
This edition published 2012
Text copyright © Norbert Landa 2011
Illustrations copyright © Jane Chapman 2011
Visit Jane Chapman at www.ChapmanandWarnes.com
Norbert Landa and Jane Chapman have asserted their rights to be
identified as the author and illustrator of this work under the
Copyright, Designs and Patents Act, 1988
A CIP catalogue record for this book is
available from the British Library
All rights reserved
ISBN: 978-1-84895-143-3
Printed in China
LTP/1900/0883/0314

2 4 6 8 10 9 7 5 3

The Slurpy Burpy Bear

Norbert Landa

Jane Chapman

LITTLE TIGER PRESS

London

Big Bear noisily slurped his mushroom
stew and happily chomped and burped.
"This is the one good thing about being
the One and Only Bear!" he thought.
"I can eat the way I like!"

CRUNCH! CHOMP! BURP!

Across the river Little Rabbit's ears twitched. What was that terrible, crunching, roaring sound?

"Hush!" Mama Rabbit whispered. "That is the Beast's horrible sound!"

SLURP! YUM YUM!

"The Beast?" Little Rabbit asked.

"Oh, yes!" Uncle Rabbit said
fearfully. "The Beast – with its
beastly paws and frightful fangs!"

"And HUGE eerie ears!"
Aunt Rabbit added.

"We all must hush and hide!"
Papa Rabbit told Little Rabbit,
"or the Beast will get us!"

Big Bear gulped down his honey and had a last, big burp. And as he got up, his botty let out a trumpy tune. Ooops!

Paaaaa

"The Beast is roaring! Hide, Little Rabbit!"
Papa Rabbit shrieked. "And hold your
breath – or you will faint from the
Beast's evil stink!"

Trembling, the rabbits hid in
their burrow.

arp!

Sometimes, Big Bear thought of crossing the river to look for a friend. But when he dipped his toes in the cold water, he would shiver, "Brrrr, brrrr, no way!" Then he would sing:

"*I am the One and Only,*
The One and Only
Lonely Bear,
With no one there
for me to care . . ."
And Big Bear couldn't help crying aloud.

Hooo sobb weee sobb wooaa

"It's the Beast's wicked howling again!" Little Rabbit would whisper. "He is out on the hunt!"

One day, as Big Bear
scratched against a
big, old tree . . .

SNAP!

Snap! the tree
cracked and fell
across the river.

"I've built a bridge!" Big Bear
said proudly. "Now I can look for
a friend!" He brushed down his
fur and set off.

Across the river, Little Rabbit was
chasing butterflies in the wood.
"You'd better hide!" he roared,
"for I'm the Beast!"
Then suddenly . . .

CRASH!

. . . Little Rabbit bumped into something big, soft and furry. From high above he heard a deep and friendly voice saying: "Hey, who's that down there?"

"I'm Little Rabbit,"
Little Rabbit said as strong
arms lifted him up.
"Oh my! You are so big!"
"That's because I am Big Bear,"
Big Bear smiled. "Are there more
of you here?"
"Oh, yes!" Little Rabbit said.
"But we always hide from the Beast!"
"Beast?" Big Bear asked. "What Beast?"

So Little Rabbit told Big Bear all
about the Beast's . . .

battle **roaring**,

and **wicked howling**,

and **frightful fangs**,

and **sinister stink**.

"Well, I've never seen any Beast,"
Big Bear said.

"That's because you are so big!" cried
Little Rabbit. "The Beast hides from *you!*"

"Yes!" Big Bear said proudly. "Perhaps
I could protect you?"

"Oh, yes, please!" Little
Rabbit cheered.

So Big Bear carefully
put Little Rabbit on his
mighty shoulders, and
off they stamped.

Papa Rabbit nearly fell over in shock when he saw Little Rabbit. He hammered against Big Bear's belly.

"Don't you dare do Little Rabbit any harm!" he cried.

"Don't worry, Papi!" Little Rabbit called. "Big Bear is my friend. He has promised to protect us from the Beast!"

"Can you really protect us?" Mama Rabbit asked.

"Yes, I can!" Big Bear answered with a smile. He let everyone feel his muscles and sit on his paws.

"Hurray!" the rabbits cheered. "Stay with us, Big Bear!"

So Big Bear stayed, and soon the rabbits forgot all about the beast. Only sometimes, faint sounds reminded them of something . . .

"You must never do this with others around you," Big Bear whispered to Little Rabbit.

And they giggled together.

SLURP! SLURP! BURP!

As for Big Bear . . .

BUI

. . . he was so happy to be no longer
the One and Only Lonely Bear.
   And when it was time to sleep,
he would snuggle up with the
rabbits and sing to himself:
   "I am no longer lonely,
   I am the one who's only
      a big and happy bear,
   My little friends around
      may slumber safe and sound,
   Because they know I'm there."

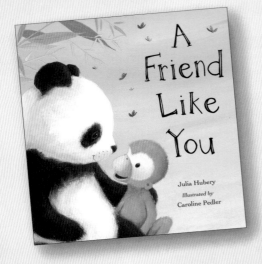

A
Friend
Like
You

Julia Hubery

Illustrated by
Caroline Pedler

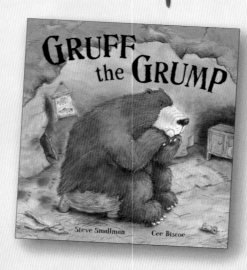

GRUFF
the GRUMP

Steve Smallman   Cee Biscoe

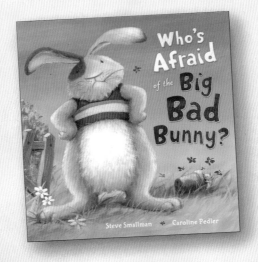

Who's
Afraid
of the Big
Bad
Bunny?

Steve Smallman   Caroline Pedler

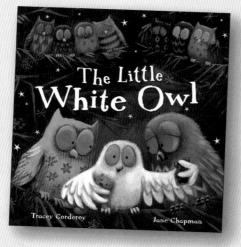

The Little
WHITE OWL

Tracey Corderoy   Jane Chapman

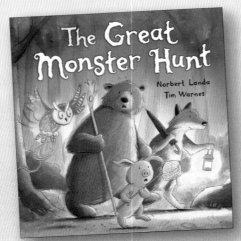

The Great
Monster Hunt

Norbert Landa
Tim Warnes

Tracey Corderoy   Gavin Scott

Little Penguin
LOST

More loveable books
from Little Tiger Press!

For information regarding any of the above titles
or for our catalogue, please contact us:
Little Tiger Press, 1 The Coda Centre,
189 Munster Road, London SW6 6AW
Tel: 020 7385 6333 • Fax: 020 7385 7333
E-mail: contact@littletiger.co.uk
www.littletiger.co.uk

This **Little Tiger** book belongs to:

For Mark, with my love xx – T C

To the lovely Gu – G S

LITTLE TIGER PRESS
1 The Coda Centre, 189 Munster Road, London SW6 6AW
www.littletiger.co.uk
First published in Great Britain 2011 as *Brave Little Penguin*
This edition published 2012
Text copyright © Tracey Corderoy 2011 • Illustrations copyright © Gavin Scott 2011
Tracey Corderoy and Gavin Scott have asserted their rights to be identified
as the author and illustrator of this work under the Copyright,
Designs and Patents Act, 1988
A CIP catalogue record for this book is
available from the British Library
All rights reserved
ISBN 978-1-84895-244-7
Printed in China
LTP/1900/0883/0314

2 4 6 8 10 9 7 5 3

Little Penguin
LOST

Tracey Corderoy   Gavin Scott

LITTLE TIGER PRESS
London

Three little roly-poly penguins were having their afternoon snack. Percy and Posy were eating up nicely. But Plip was too busy playing with his favourite toy.

"Hey, Plip," said Percy. "Finish your fish or Wal-the-Wump will snap it up."

"Who's scared of a grumpy old walrus?" giggled Plip. "Not me!"

After their snack, it was swim-time.
But Plip had to keep his toy dry.
   "Oh, Plip!" sighed Posy. "Swim like
us or one day Wal-the-Wump might
catch you."
   "Wal-the-Wump?" giggled Plip.
"He doesn't scare me!"

When the penguins were too shivery to swim anymore, they played Wal-the-Wump games instead.

"Raggh!" growled Posy.
"I'm Wal. And I'm coming to get you!"

"My turn!" cried Plip, wobbling uphill
and trying to look big and scary.
"I'm Wal-the-Wump and I'll squash
you flat! Hee hee!"

They played together all afternoon.
Then, suddenly, Plip went quiet.
"Hungry?" asked Posy.
"Sleepy?" Percy said.
But Plip just opened his beak
and wailed . . .

"WHERE'S MY SOCKYBUG?"

Everyone searched for
Plip's little sock toy.
   They checked under
the water . . .

then inside all
the caves.

"Where can he be?" sighed Plip.
"He'll be wanting a cuddle."

They were still searching when big snow clouds
gathered and the sky grew dark and stormy.
Percy put a wing around Plip's shoulder.
"You're a big boy now," he said. "You don't
need a baby toy, do you?"

"But he's not a toy," sniffed Plip.
"He's my friend."

They were just about to head back
home when: "Wait!" cried Plip.
"I think I know where I left him!"
He shot away over the hill as
snow began to fall.
"Sockybug!" he called . . .

"I'm coming to get you!"

Percy and Posy raced after Plip
through the tumbling snow.
"Come back!" they yelled.
Then, suddenly, Percy gave a
great gasp, "Oh no!"

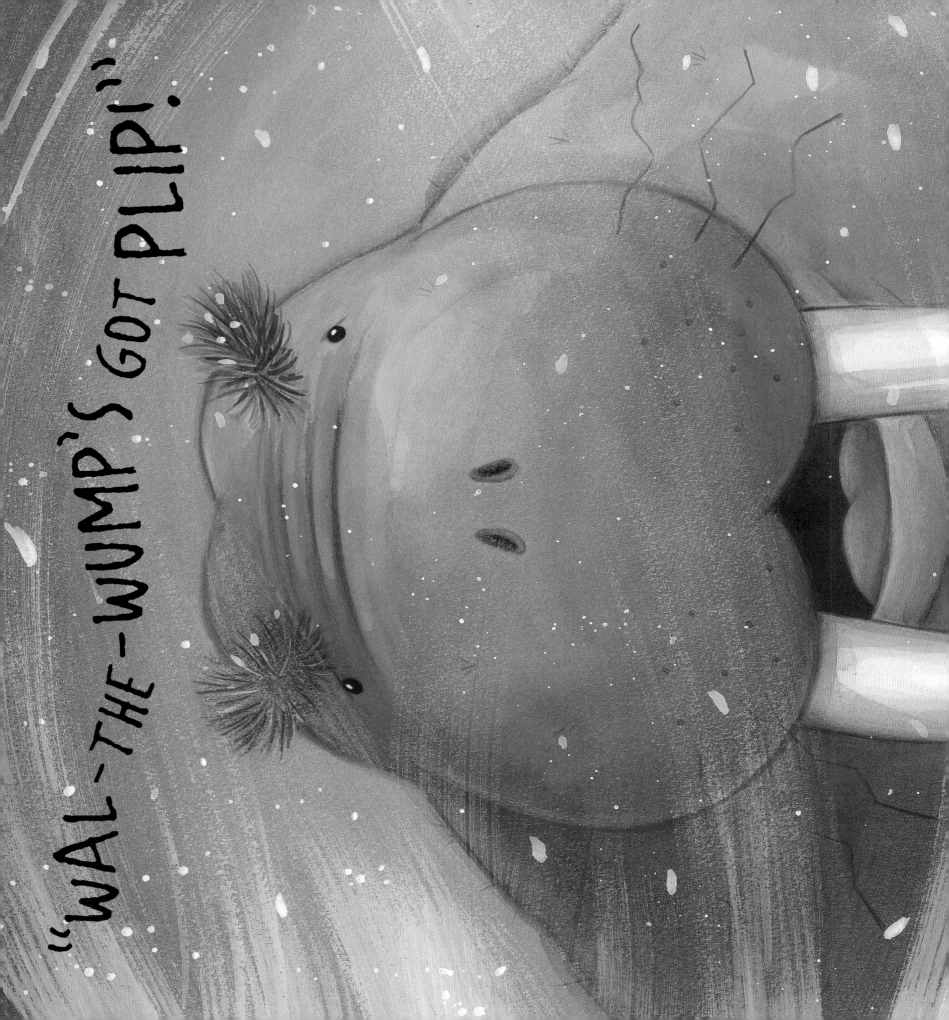

The walrus's enormous teeth
flashed as his jaws opened wide . . .

And Wal let out a gigantic guffaw.
"Tickle, tickle!" chuckled Plip.
Then he turned to his brother and
sister. "Wal found my Sockybug
– look!" he cried.

"HO, HO,

HO!"

"Tickle, tickle!"

After that, Plip made everyone
their very own Sockybugs.
And from then on, tickle-time
was the best time of the day!

Get lost in another book
from Little Tiger

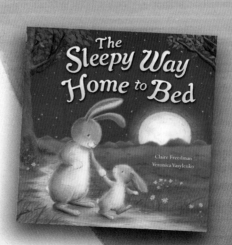

For information regarding any of the above titles
or for our catalogue, please contact us:
Little Tiger Press, 1 The Coda Centre, 189 Munster Road, London SW6 6AW
Tel: 020 7385 6333 • Fax: 020 7385 7333
E-mail: contact@littletiger.co.uk • www.littletiger.co.uk